THIS CANDLEWICK BOOK BELONGS TO:

_____

_____

_____

To Melissa, Oliver, and Pumpkin
C. F.

For Floyd the Brooklyn alley-cat
J. M.

First paperback edition 2018

The Library of Congress has cataloged the hardcover edition as follows:
Friend, Catherine.
The perfect nest / Catherine Friend ; illustrated by John Manders.
p.   cm.
Summary: Jack the cat gets much more than he bargained for when
he decides to build the perfect nest to attract the perfect chicken.
ISBN 978-0-7636-2430-9 (hardcover)
[1. Cats–Fiction.   2. Chickens–Fiction.
3. Nests–Fiction.   4. Domestic animals–Fiction.]
I. Manders, John, ill. II. Title.
PZ7.F91523Per 2007
[E]–dc22   2006047518

ISBN 978-0-7636-9975-8 (paperback)

20 21 22 23 CCP 10 9 8 7 6 5 4 3

Printed in Shenzhen, Guangdong, China

This book was typeset in Cafeteria.
The illustrations were done in gouache.

Candlewick Press
99 Dover Street
Somerville, Massachusetts 02144

visit us at www.candlewick.com

The Perfect Nest

Catherine Friend

illustrated by John Manders

CANDLEWICK PRESS

Jack the cat gathered together everything he needed, then built the perfect nest—dry and cozy and just the right size.

But the nest was not for Jack. With this perfect nest, he would attract a perfect chicken, who would lay a perfect egg, which would make a perfect omelet for a cat like Jack.

Soon enough, a chicken came along.

"¡Caramba!" she cried. "A perfect nest."
She hopped up and laid a small egg.

Then a duck waddled by.

"Sacré bleu!" she cried.

"Zee perfect nest."

The duck pushed the chicken out, hopped up, and laid a medium-size egg.

Then a goose lumbered by.

"Great balls of fire!" she cried. "A perfect nest."

The goose pushed the duck out, hopped up, and laid a large egg.

Jack's mouth began to water.

Three eggs would make
three omelets.

But then the duck leaped onto the goose's back.

"Zees ees my nest."

The chicken flew up onto the duck.

"No, this is *my* nest."

The three cackled and quacked and honked, but each refused to leave the perfect nest. They squished each other for days.

Each day, Jack tried to get the birds off the eggs.

"Fire! Fire!"
he cried.

They didn't move.

"Flood! Flood!"

he cried.

They didn't move.

"Wolf! Wolf!"

he cried.

But the chicken, the duck, and the goose **would not move.**

Finally, Jack stood before them. "You birds are so silly. The next farm over has an even better nest, and it's empty. Why doesn't one of you use that nest?"

"An empty nest?" cried the chicken. "Without a goose to sit on my head? ¡Caramba!"

"Sacré bleu!" cried the duck. "I am tired of smelling like zee chicken. Zat nest ees mine!"

"Great balls of fire!" cried the goose. "Outta my way!"

And they all flapped away.

Alone at last, Jack returned to the nest and peeked inside. He arranged the eggs neatly in a row: small breakfast, medium lunch, and large dinner. Jack's stomach rumbled.

But then . . .

CRACK!

The small egg broke open and out popped a wet baby chick, who looked up at Jack and said, "¡Caramba! ¡Hola, Mamá!"

CRACKETY-SNAP!

The medium-size egg broke open and out scrambled a wet baby duck, who looked up at Jack and said, "Sacré bleu! Bonjour, Maman."

CRACKETY-
CRACKETY
BOOM!

The largest egg broke open and out stepped a wet baby goose,
who looked up at Jack and said, "Great balls of fire! Howdy, Ma."

Jack stared at the babies. What was he to do? He couldn't make omelets out of *them.*

"Dry me, dry me, dry me," cried the soggy baby chick.

"Feed me, feed me, feed me," cried the hungry baby duck.

"Play, play, play," cried the excited baby goose.

Jack hid in the barn.
The three babies
found him.

He hid in the woods.
The three babies found him.

Jack hid under the tractor.

The three babies found him and dragged him back to the nest.

"Sleep, sleep, sleep," the tired babies finally whispered.

"Cold, cold, cold," said the shivering babies.

Jack scratched his head. Someone had to care for these babies, but there was no one else around.

Jack lifted all three babies into the nest.

"Buenas noches, Mamá," said the baby chick.

"Bonne nuit, Maman," said the baby duck.

"Sweet dreams, Ma," said the baby goose.

Then Jack climbed into the nest, and the babies fell asleep. That's when he realized that this really was the perfect nest.

Catherine Friend is the author of the acclaimed memoir *Hit By a Farm: How I Learned to Stop Worrying and Love the Barn*, as well as two Brand New Readers, *Funny Ruby* and *Eddie the Raccoon*. On her farm in southeastern Minnesota she once had a duck and a chicken who insisted on sharing a nest. The author likes spending time at home, which is for her, she says, "the perfect nest."

John Manders has illustrated many children's books, including *Where's My Mummy?* and *Henry and the Buccaneer Bunnies*. He lives in Oil City, Pennsylvania, with his wife, two dogs, and a parrot who loves to build nests out of cardboard (but has never laid an egg). "The illustrations for this book took a long time to paint," the artist says, "because every so often I had to stop and make myself an omelet."